ALTERNATOR BOOKS™

UNEXPLAINED

SCARY ALIEN ABDUCTIONS

Craig Boutland

Lerner Publications ◆ Minneapolis

Lerner Publications Company
A division of Lerner Publishing Group, Inc.
241 First Avenue North
Minneapolis, MN 55401 USA

For reading levels and more information, look up this title at www.lernerbooks.com.

Main body text set in Minion Pro.
Font provided by Adobe Systems.

Library of Congress Cataloging-in-Publication Data

Names: Boutland, Craig, author.
Title: Scary alien abductions / Craig Boutland.
Description: Minneapolis : Lerner Publications, 2019. | Series: Unexplained (Alternator Books™) | Includes bibliographical references and index.
Identifiers: LCCN 2018057297 (print) | LCCN 2019008784 (ebook) | ISBN 9781541562875 (eb pdf) | ISBN 9781541562844 (lb : alk. paper) | ISBN 9781541573772 (pb : alk. paper)
Subjects: LCSH: Alien abduction—Juvenile literature. | Human-alien encounters—Juvenile literature.
Classification: LCC BF2050 (ebook) | LCC BF2050 .B68 2019 (print) | DDC 001.942—dc23

LC record available at https://lccn.loc.gov/2018057297

Manufactured in the United States of America
1-46410-47500-4/5/2019

Contents

Introduction 4
Aliens and Antonio Vilas-Boas 6
Betty and Barney Hill 12
New Abduction Stories 18
Real Or Imagined? 24
Glossary 30
Further Information 31
Index 32

Introduction

Thousands of Americans have reported being captured by aliens. There have been similar stories from other countries too. It seems impossible to believe that aliens from other planets have visited Earth and kidnapped people. But what else could explain the strange experiences people have described?

The stories all seem to have things in common. Alien creatures are usually described as having big eyes. Sometimes they speak. The people they capture are often given a tour of the spacecraft. They are also physically examined. It's not surprising that people who have been **abducted** say they were terrified. After their experience, some found it hard to live a normal life again.

Aliens and Antonio Vilas-Boas

One of the first stories to be taken seriously was that of Antonio Vilas-Boas, the son of a Brazilian farmer. One hot night in 1957, Antonio was out on his tractor plowing fields. He suddenly saw a strange aircraft land nearby. It was round and lowered three legs to support itself when it landed. Antonio was scared and began to drive away, but the tractor's engine stopped.

Capture

Antonio tried to run, but a small, humanlike being wearing a helmet rushed toward him. The first alien was joined by three more. They grabbed hold of Antonio. He was dragged into the strange aircraft. Antonio said he thought the aliens were about five feet (1.5 m) tall.

Antonio saw symbols above one of the doors in the spacecraft. He memorized the symbols and drew them for investigators.

Inside the Ship

Antonio's clothes were taken away. He was examined by some of the aliens. They took a sample of his blood. He remembered that one of the doors he was taken through had lettering above it. He did not recognize the language. Then Antonio was left in a room that filled with a gas that made him ill.

One of the aliens had cat-like features and long white hair. Its eyes were very big. Antonio was given his clothes back and taken on a tour of the spacecraft. He tried to steal some kind of clock or measuring device, but the aliens stopped him. Four hours after he was taken, he was allowed to leave the spacecraft. Then the craft flew off.

Radiation Sickness

After his experience, Antonio lost his appetite. He suffered from **nausea** and weakness. He also had headaches. Whenever he had a bruise, it turned into a large sore. A doctor who examined him thought Antonio had been exposed to **radiation**. Something had definitely happened to him. But could he really have been taken up into an alien spaceship?

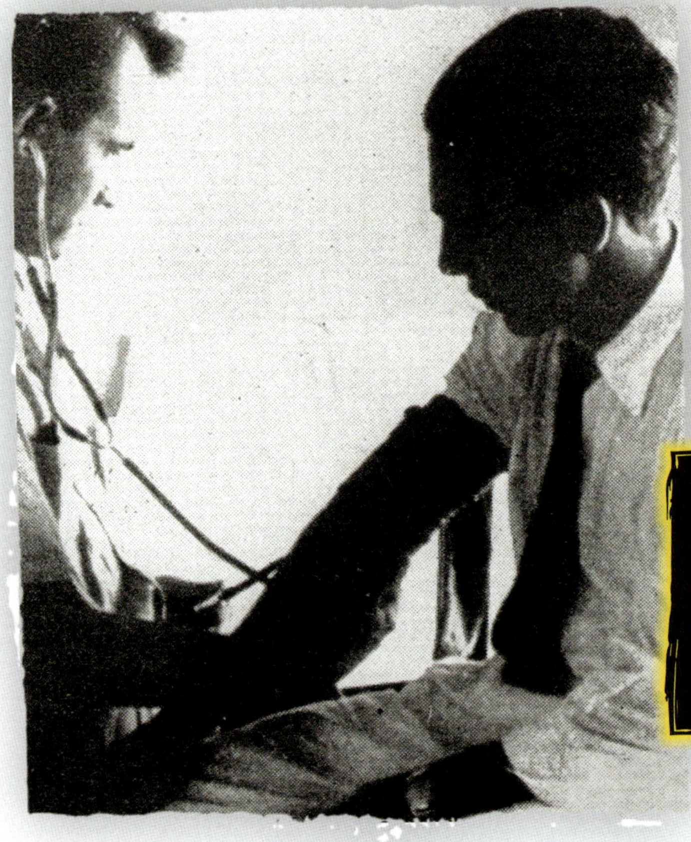

A doctor examined Antonio Vilas-Boas. He thought Antonio's illnesses were caused by exposure to radiation.

No Explanation

Antonio Vilas-Boas stuck to his story until he died in 1991. Some people thought that he made everything up using details from stories he had read. But the health problems he suffered from were real. Could he have been telling the truth after all?

Betty and Barney Hill

Betty and Barney Hill claimed to have been abducted by aliens in September of 1961. Something strange had happened to the Hills while they were on their way home from a vacation in Canada. Their story became famous. At first they couldn't remember anything. The details were filled in over several years.

Betty and Barney were driving along a dark road in New Hampshire when they saw a strange bright light in the sky. They thought it was a star. They looked at it for a while. Then a huge round spacecraft appeared. It hovered in front of their car, forcing them to stop. They tried to drive off. Instead, they suddenly found themselves 35 miles (56 km) further down the road.

Barney and Betty Hill described the size and shape of the flying saucer to investigators.

Over the next few nights, Betty had dreams about the car stopping at a roadblock. Strange, short creatures took her inside a spacecraft. She was given a medical examination. One of the creatures cut off some of her hair, and a needle was inserted into her stomach. A researcher interviewed the Hills in October 1961. He said he thought they were telling the truth. Something strange had happened to them.

Where Did the Aliens Come From?

Over the next two years, Barney became anxious. He met with a **psychiatrist**. In 1964 Barney agreed to try **hypnosis**. He remembered more details about his abduction. Betty was also hypnotized, and she remembered more than she had been able to before. She even remembered an alien showing her a map of the stars.

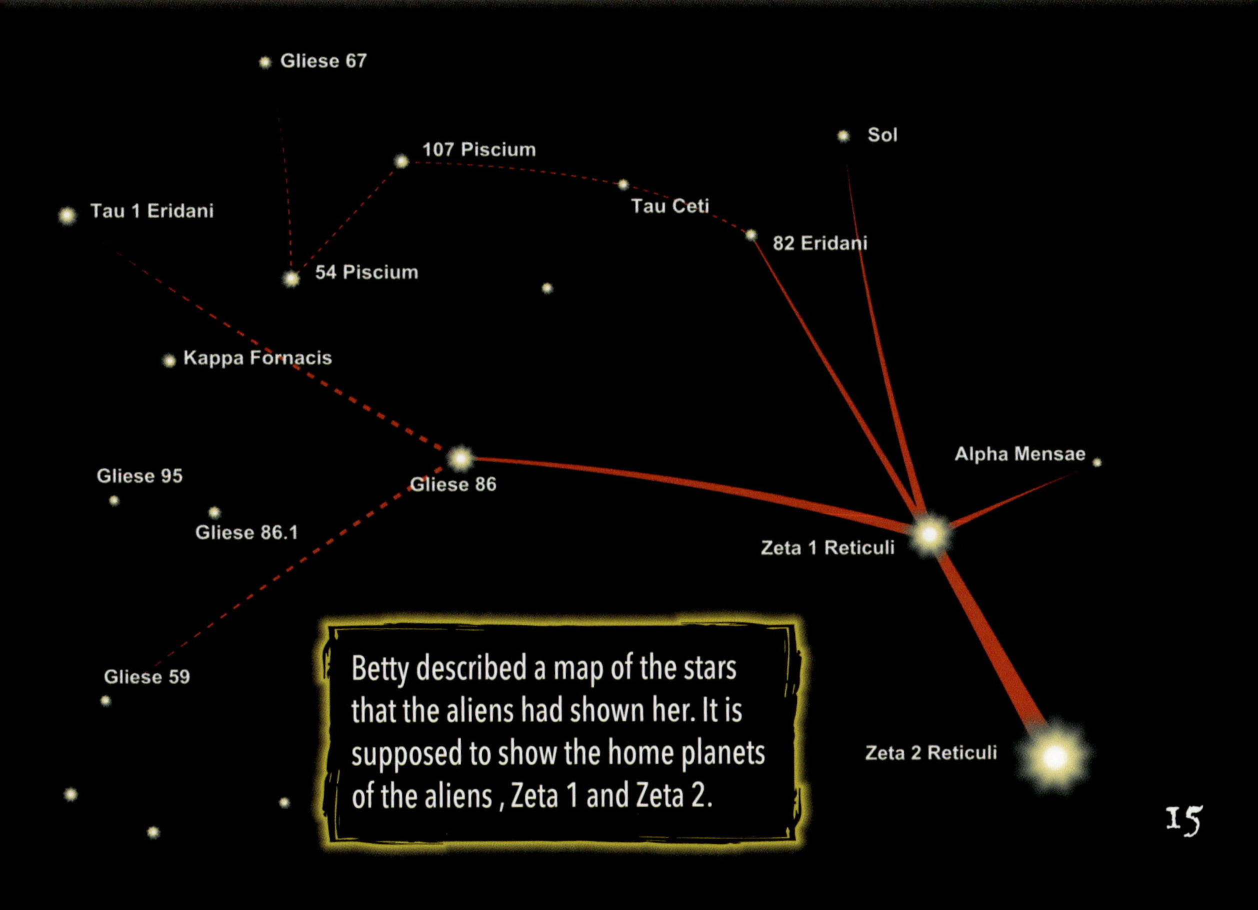

Betty described a map of the stars that the aliens had shown her. It is supposed to show the home planets of the aliens , Zeta 1 and Zeta 2.

Just a Story?

The hypnotist who examined Barney and Betty was Dr. Benjamin Simon. Unlike the researcher who spoke to them in 1961, Dr. Simon thought their story was a **fantasy**. He did not think they had been kidnapped by aliens. However, he thought Barney and Betty both believed they were telling the truth.

Dr. Benjamin Simon put Barney and Betty Hill into a **trance** to see if they could remember any more about their encounter in September 1961.

Although Dr. Simon did not believe in aliens or **unidentified** flying objects (UFOs), he saw that the hypnosis sessions had helped with Barney's anxiety. The Hills went on to live their regular lives. Barney died in 1969 at the age of forty-six, but Betty continued to report other alien encounters and UFO sightings later in life. She passed away in 2004.

New Abduction Stories

People have been reporting encounters with aliens for more than seventy years. However, space exploration has not found any evidence of aliens living on other planets. People who believe in aliens say that is because the aliens come from unknown planets. In the 1980s and 1990s, many more stories about aliens appeared.

Similar Stories

Like Betty and Barney Hill, other people who had been abducted said there were periods of time that they could not remember. What happened during these abductions also followed a similar pattern. The aliens took the humans into a spacecraft, where they were examined.

Some people said the aliens had talked to them. They said they were given information. Sometimes the information was sent **telepathically**, so there was no difficulty with language. Often there was a trip into space. The abducted people described looking at Earth from the spaceship.

Where Am I?

The return to normal life was confusing for all the **abductees**. They woke up to find themselves somewhere they had not expected to be. Often several hours had gone by, but it seemed that no time had passed at all. Only later did the memories of the abduction come back. Sometimes they came back in dreams.

These stories about alien abductions showed that something strange was going on. It seemed that the minds of people had somehow been taken over. If the stories were to be believed, aliens were controlling the memories of the abductees. Their memories were often terrifying. Some abductees believed they had been specially chosen to receive important information from the aliens who controlled their memories.

Conspiracy Theory

Some people believe that it is the US government, not aliens, who are controlling their minds. They believe they were abducted by a secret government organization and had **microchips** inserted into their brains. However, there is no evidence to support such a **conspiracy theory**.

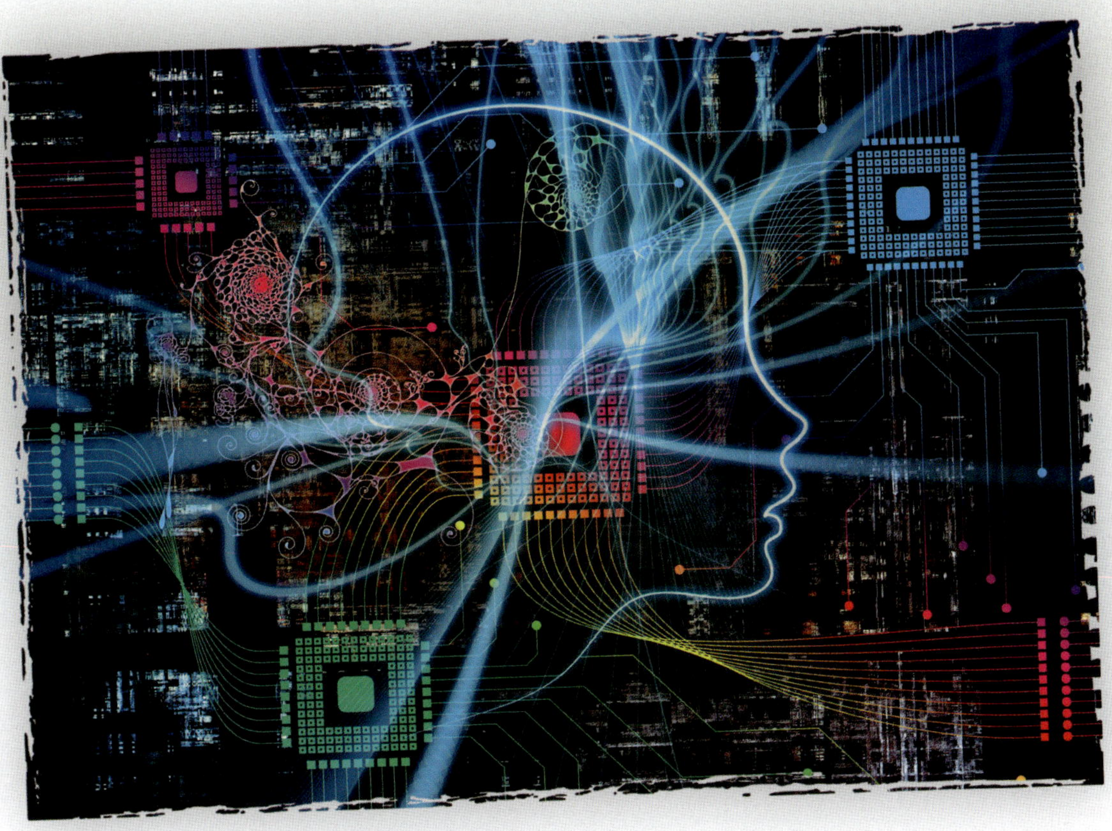

Real Or Imagined?

It is hard to imagine how spacecraft could land in the United States without being spotted. The military watches for any aircraft entering US air space. There have been no reports of anything unusual. This may be because alien spacecraft block the radio waves used by radar. Some people think that the US government itself is involved in some way. However, there may be other explanations.

Psychiatrists have examined people who say they were abducted. They usually report that the people do not have any mental illness. However, they appear to have symptoms that are similar to post-traumatic stress disorder (PTSD). This is a condition caused by highly stressful events such as wartime combat, national disaster, or physical violence. It can cause depression, anxiety, nightmares, and memory loss.

Observatories in New Mexico use satellite dishes and radio telescopes to look into space. No sightings of alien spacecraft have been reported.

Medical Explanations?

Harvard University did a study on people who said they were abducted. Psychiatrists found the people had certain things in common. They often suffered from sleep paralysis. This is when people wake up and are aware of their surroundings but are unable to move or speak. It is a frightening experience.

Some scientists think that rapid eye movement while we are asleep represents a change of scene in our dreams.

There are several stages of sleep. When people are in the sleep stage called **REM**, it feels like being awake. Dreams appear to be real. If we acted out our dreams, we might harm ourselves. So, our muscles become so relaxed that we cannot move. Sleep paralysis happens when we wake up during this type of sleep. REM dreams can be remembered. But it does not mean they were real.

There was an increase in alien abduction stories after the release of the film *Close Encounters of the Third Kind* (1977).

Researchers and psychiatrists think sleep paralysis could be the answer to the mystery of alien abductions. People's feelings of fear during sleep paralysis may have become confused with their memories of watching films about UFOs and aliens. After the success of the film *Close Encounters of the Third Kind*, people began to wonder if there could actually be aliens in outer space. They might have had dreams about being abducted by aliens while suffering from sleep paralysis.

Do You Believe in Aliens?

Some people really believe that they have met or been abducted by aliens. Perhaps they have false memories. This means that people have memories of things they have imagined but believe to be real.

There are many reasons to doubt accounts about visiting aliens. But the truth is that we don't really know if aliens exist somewhere in outer space.

Glossary

abducted: kidnapped or taken away by force

abductees: people who have been abducted

conspiracy theory: a theory that explains an event or situation as being the result of a secret plot

fantasy: something that is imagined or unreal

hypnosis: when a person is put into a sleep-like state to help them remember things

microchips: very small electronic circuits made from silicon that hold large amounts of information

nausea: a feeling of sickness and a desire to vomit

psychiatrist: a specialist in psychiatry, a branch of medicine that deals with disorders of the mind, emotions, or behavior

radiation: energy that moves from one place to another. There are different kinds of radiation. Electromagnetic, mechanical, nuclear, and radiation given off by cosmic rays.

REM: the rapid eye movement stage of sleep. This is the light stage of sleep when people dream.

telepathically: knowledge passed from one person to another by direct exchange of thoughts, without the need for speech

trance: a sleep-like state that can be caused by hypnosis

unidentified: when it is not known what something is

Further Information

Betty and Barney Hill Abduction
https://www.historicmysteries.com/betty-and-barney-hill-abduction/

Five Traits That Could Get You "Abducted by Aliens"
https://www.psychologytoday.com/gb/blog/why-we-worry/201207/five-traits-could-get-you-abducted-aliens

Johnson, C. M. *Close Encounters.* Fremont, CA: Full Tilt Press, 2018

Levete, Sarah. *Aliens and UFOs.* New York: Gareth Stevens Publishing, 2017.

Kenney, Karen. *Mysterious UFOs and Aliens.* Minneapolis: Lerner Publications, 2018.

What Exactly Are UFOs?
https://www.cbc.ca/kidscbc2/the-feed/what-exactly-are-ufos

When Did Alien Sightings Turn into Alien Abductions?
https://www.airspacemag.com/daily-planet/when-did-alien-sightings-turn-alien-abductions-180967397/

Index

abductees 4–5, 7, 12–17, 19–23, 25–26, 29

conspiracy 23

Hill, Betty and Barney 12–17, 19

hypnosis 15–16

microchips 23

post-traumatic stress disorder 25

psychiatrist 15, 25–26, 28

radiation 10

REM 27

Simon, Benjamin 16–17

sleep paralysis 26–28

star map 15

telepathic communication 20

US government 23, 24

Vilas-Boas, Antonio 6–11

Photo acknowledgments

The images inside this book are used with permission of: ©Shutterstock/donates, p. 1; ©Shutterstock /M. Cornelius, p. 4-5; ©iStockphoto.com/Martinelli73, p. 6-7; ©Topfoto / Fortean, p. 8; ©iStockphoto.com/Rastan, p. 9; ©Topfoto/Fortean, p. 10; ©iStockphoto.com/ stocksnapper, p. 11; ©Shutterstock/Sergey Molchenko, p. 12-13; ©Topfoto/The Granger Collection, p. 14; ©Brown Bear Books, p. 15; © ©iStockphoto.com/joelclak, p. 16; ©Alamy/ Charles Walker Collection, p. 17; ©Shutterstock /Fer Gregory, p. 18-19; ©iStockphoto.com/ dotted hippo, p. 20; ©iStockphoto.com/Katarzyna Bialaslweicz, p. 21; ©iStockphoto/nullplus, p. 22; ©Shutterstock/Andrew Ags, p. 23; ©iStockphoto.com/Pglam, p. 24-25; ©iStockphoto. com/Antonio Guilliem, p. 26; ©Science Photo Library/Alan Hobson, p. 27; ©Alamy/Everett Collection Inc, p. 28; ©iStockphoto.com/cosmin4000, p. 29.

Front Cover: ©iStockphoto.com/cosmin4000

Brown Bear Books has made every attempt to contact the copyright holder. If anyone has any information please contact licensing@brownbear.co.uk